Weekly Reader Children's Book Club

presents

One Kitten for Kim

An Addisonian Press Book

The Addison-Wesley Publishing Company, Inc.

Library of Congress catalog card number 69-15799
Printed in the United States of America

Weekly Reader Children's Book Club Edition
Primary Division

ONE Kitten FOR Kim

By Adelaide Holl

illustrated by DON MADDEN

Addison-Wesley Publishing Company, Inc.

Reading, Massachusetts

im had a cat named Geraldine and seven kittens. One kitten was striped like a tiny tiger. One was round, and soft, and white as a snowball. Two were black as a midnight sky, and three had black and white polka-dots all over.

Kim thought that having seven kittens was fun. Kim's mother and father did not agree.

"There are too many cats in this house," said Kim's father one day. "You may keep Geraldine and one kitten. You will have to give the others away."

"Yes," agreed Kim's mother. "Two pets are enough in one house."

Kim chose the roundest and rolliest polka-dot kitten for his own. He put the others in his mother's laundry basket and set the basket in his yellow wagon. Away he went down the street with SIX kittens in his basket.

Mrs. McGinty, who lived next door, was sweeping her sidewalk. "What's in your basket, Kim?" she asked with interest.

"Kittens," Kim told her. "Would you like one for a pet?"

"I *am* rather lonely," said Mrs. McGinty, "and a kitten would keep me company. I have two goldfish, but goldfish are not very good company. A kitten would curl up in my lap and purr. Goldfish cannot do that."

Mrs. McGinty lifted up a snowball-white kitten and stroked its silky fur. Then she said, "But what will I do with my goldfish? A kitten will grow up to be a cat. A cat will eat goldfish."

"You could give the goldfish to me," said Kim brightly.

Mrs. McGinty hurried into the house, and she came out carrying a round, glass bowl. Inside the bowl, two golden-orange fish were swimming around and around. They had shiny fins. They had tails like little waving fans. Their mouths were like tiny, round *o*'s.

Kim thanked Mrs.McGinty. Then he set the glass bowl in his wagon, and away he went down the street with

FIVE kittens in his basket

and two  in a

Kim pulled his wagon slowly, because the water in the goldfish bowl went *slish-slosh-splash*. He pulled his wagon quietly, because he was coming to Miss Murphy's house. Miss Murphy did not like noise. She did not like rattley wagons, or squeaky wheels, or noisy children. Miss Murphy sat on her front porch quietly rocking.

shhh!

"Hello, Miss Murphy," said Kim politely. "I have some kittens to give away. Nice QUIET ones," he added.

"Did you say QUIET kittens?" asked Miss Murphy with interest. "Let me see them."

She peered into the basket. The kittens were curled into soft balls. They were making quiet purring sounds.

"Wait here a minute, Kim," said Miss Murphy, hurrying up the steps to the door.

She came out carrying a golden cage. Inside it, sat a large green parrot, awking and squawking noisily.

"This is Skipper," she explained. "My brother, who is a sea captain, brought him to me from far across the sea. Skipper is a very noisy bird. He chatters, and he whistles, and he sings *The Sailor's Hornpipe*. I simply can't stand noisy pets! Would you trade one of your nice quiet kittens for a nice noisy parrot?"

Kim was delighted. Miss Murphy chose a round polka-dot kitten that was curled up quietly asleep.

Kim took the awking, squawking parrot and set the cage carefully in the wagon. He thanked Miss Murphy. Then away he went down the street with

FOUR kittens in his basket

two  in a

and one green in a

Kim turned the corner and stopped in front of Mr. Wiggins' store. Mr. Wiggins was making bright pyramids of oranges and red apples on his fruit stand. He looked a little bit cross.

"What's the matter, Mr. Wiggins?" asked Kim.

"It's those pesky mice!" exclaimed Mr. Wiggins. "They keep nibbling my fruits and cheeses."

"What you need is a cat," said Kim. "I could give you a *kitten*. It will grow up to be a cat, and a cat will chase away the mice."

Mr. Wiggins smiled. "I could use *two* kittens," he said. He picked up the two kittens as black as a midnight sky. Then he said, "Come with me, Kim. I have something to show you."

In the back of the store there was a box with four wiggly brown puppies inside.

"Would you like to have one, Kim?" asked Mr. Wiggins.

"Sure, thanks!" said Kim with a wide grin.

He chose the puppy with the silkiest fur, the floppiest ears, and the droopiest tail. He put the puppy in a small box, set the box in his wagon, and away he went down the street with

TWO kittens in his basket

two in a

one green in a

and a wiggly brown in a

Kim turned right at the next corner and stopped to watch Mr. Green, who was working on his chicken yard. *Rap, rap, rap!* went Mr. Green's hammer.

"Those are nice chickens you have," said Kim in a friendly voice.

Mr. Green stopped hammering and looked around. "The hens are nice," he said. They give me fresh white eggs every day. But I'm going to get rid of that pesky rooster. Every morning, very early, he crows and wakes me up. I think we'll put him in the soup pot!"

"Oh, don't do that!" cried Kim. "Give him to me! Then, I'll give you a kitten."

Mr. Green looked into the basket and smiled. "That's a fine idea," he said. "My little girl has a birthday to-morrow. I'll bet she'd love this polka-dot kitten for a birthday present."

Mr. Green chased a shiny black rooster around the chicken yard until he caught him. He put the rooster into a small crate and set the crate in Kim's wagon.

"Thanks, Mr. Green," called Kim as away he went down the street with

ONE kitten in his basket

two  in a

one green in a

a wiggly brown in a

and a shiny black in a

As Kim turned the next corner, he thought, "I have just one kitten left to give away." Then he saw Millicent May and her mother in the yard. Millicent was crying and looking very unhappy. Mrs. May looked a little unhappy, too.

"What's wrong with Millicent?" Kim asked.

Mrs. May sighed. "Millicent is crying because she wants a tiger for a pet. Yesterday we went to the circus. Millicent loved the tigers. She says she won't stop crying until we buy her one."

Kim had a bright idea. "I have a kitten that looks a little like a tiger. Maybe Millicent would like it."

He lifted the last kitten out of the basket. It was yellowish with black stripes. It had a little tiger face and wide green eyes. Kim put the kitten in Millicent's lap. She stopped crying and smiled a big smile.

"Tiger!" said Millicent happily, as she stroked its fur.

Mrs. May was delighted. "Why, thank you, Kim. Would you like to have the little chameleon we got at the circus? Millicent doesn't want it."

Kim peered into the glass jar. There was a tiny green animal covered with scales. It had a little pointed face and a long green tail.

"I've never seen a chameleon before," cried Kim excitedly. "Yes, thank you! I sure would like to have it!"

Carefully he set the glass jar in his wagon, and away
he went toward home with

an EMPTY basket

two  in a

one green 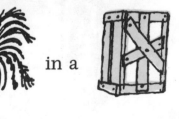 in a

a wiggly brown in a

a shiny black in a

and a tiny 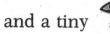 in a

As he pulled his wagon into the yard Kim shouted excitedly, "Hey, Mom, Dad! I found a home for every single kitten! Aren't you glad?"